TOMMY DONBAVAND'S FUNNY SHORTS

Duck!

WRITTEN BY TOMMY DONBAVAND
ILLUSTRATED BY PHIL CORBETT

EDGE

W FRANKLIN WATTS

LONDON·SYDNEY

Franklin Watts
First published in Great Britain in 2016 by The Watts Publishing Group

Credits
Executive Editor: Adrian Cole
Design Manager: Peter Scoulding
Cover Designer: Cathryn Gilbert
Illustrator: Phil Corbett

HB ISBN 978 1 4451 4676 8
PB ISBN 978 1 4451 4677 5
Library ebook ISBN 978 1 4451 4678 2

Printed in China

Franklin Watts
An imprint of
Hachette Children's Group
Part of The Watts Publishing Group
Carmelite House
50 Victoria Embankment
London EC4Y 0DZ

An Hachette UK Company
www.hachette.co.uk

www.franklinwatts.co.uk

Contents

Chapter One: Bench

It was late afternoon by the time Tom and Norah reached their usual bench beside the pond in the park.

"Well, I tried it like I promised," said Tom, sitting down, "but I won't be going to bingo with you again after today."

"Why not?" asked Norah, sitting beside him. "I thought you'd enjoyed it. You won ten pounds for getting a line."

"The game itself was alright," replied

Tom. "It's that place — full of old-age pensioners!"

"We're old-age pensioners!" Norah pointed out.

"Not like them, we're not!" said Tom, reaching into his bag for the loaf of stale bread they'd brought with them. "I'm young inside! Sprightly and energetic! Not like those coffin dodgers."

7

"Sprightly?" scoffed Norah. "Is that why you put your back out buttering your toast this morning?"

"That was different," Tom said, frowning at the bread. "And, talking of toast, is this the same type of bread we had at breakfast?"

"The very same, why?"

"I didn't like it," said Tom. "It tasted weird." He tore a chunk off and tossed it to the ducks waiting at the water's edge.

"Omega 33," said Norah, taking a few chunks for herself.

"Omega what?" said Tom. "Is that one of your fancy bingo calls? Like 'two little ducks, 22'."

"Don't be daft!" said Norah. "It's a vitamin, or something. Makes you dead brainy, so they say. They've started putting it in the bread."

Tom peered at the ingredients on the side of the wrapper. Omega 33 was near the top of the list. "Bread that makes you brainy?" he chuckled. "I've never heard of anything so stupid. Why can't they just make a good, old-fashioned loaf like they used to? Stop messing around with stuff."

"Well, the ducks seem to be enjoying it..." Norah said, gesturing to the pond.

Tom leaned forward and lifted his glasses. His wife was right — the ducks were fighting over the genetically modified bread, hungrily gobbling down every last crumb. "Well, they're welcome to it. I can't stand the taste."

"So, what will you be having for breakfast tomorrow?" asked Norah.

Tom shrugged. "Cornflakes, I suppose. Unless they've pumped them full of muck, too."

He ripped off another chunk and tossed it into the water, causing a mini-riot among the waiting ducks.

"That fella, the one with the weed stuck on his beak so it looks like a moustache, he's getting most of it," Tom said.

"Then throw some further out to the little ones. A man with your energy ought to be able to do that with no trouble," Norah suggested with a wink.

"Cheeky!"

The pair fell into a comfortable silence as they finished tossing bread to their feathered audience. Then Norah helped Tom to his feet and they set off for home.

There was a single lump of wet bread left floating in the water. Had either Tom or Norah looked back at the pond, they would have spotted the duck with the moustache snatch up a stick using his feathery wing. With angry eyes, the duck stabbed the pointy end at his fellow ducks, warning them away from the mushy bread. He scoffed it down and quacked loudly.

But Tom and Norah didn't look back. They were already thinking about the lovely piece of fish they had waiting for them at home for their tea. So no one was there to see The Drake step out of the water onto the grass and throw his stick aside. He twisted his moustache with the tip of his wing as he surveyed the world of humans, and smiled...

Chapter Two: Birds

Six months later...

There were posters of The Drake hanging in every street, along with his emblem of two crossed yellow duck legs. He was the mastermind who had led the duck uprising, taking over the entire country with his feathered army. All had gone well for The Drake, but a secret human resistance force — led by a war council — was fighting back. They were determined to pluck The Drake from his secret underground nest and put

a stop to his evil plans.

Jasmine and Luke Viccars hid in the bushes and watched as a parade of almost a thousand ducks flip-flapped along the street, their webbed feet striking the ground in perfect unison. First there came three rows of green heads — the dominant males — then brown lines of those ducks in the lower ranks.

Bringing up the rear was a gaggle of geese and swans. They were trying to march in time with the ducks, but kept tripping over each other and squabbling.

"It's the Dabbler platoon," Jasmine hissed to her brother. "I recognise Colonel P. King at the front there."

"I didn't think they were supposed to

be in town for another month," said Luke, scribbling the information down in an old school notebook.

"They're not," Jasmine confirmed. "The Drake must have changed his plans..."

Thin crowds of people were gathered on the pavements, their arms held straight out, wrists pressed together and their palms opening and closing — the official salute of The Drake's invading armies.

Suddenly, a middle-aged man stepped out into the road and held up a hand, trying to stop the duck-stepping birds.

"Get back in the water!" he cried. "This world belongs to human beings!"

At the front of the platoon, Colonel

P. King raised a wing and his soldiers stopped on the spot, snapping to attention. Slowly, the duck in charge approached the trembling man, looking him up and down with piercing black eyes.

"Times have changed, my friend," the duck sneered. "Thanks to The Drake, there is a new order sweeping the world. A new feathered order!"

Luke and Jasmine watched from their hiding place in horrified silence, long used to the fact that ducks could now talk.

"Well, you won't win!" cried the man. "It won't be long before we're all back to covering you in orange sauce and eating you!"

"Guards!" screeched the Colonel.

With a series of angry honks, two geese and a swan raced up the line of soldiers to the front of the parade. The swan scurried towards the man, head raised high and wings outstretched and flapping.

"I would be careful if I were you," warned Colonel P. King. "He could easily break your arm..."

"I... I'm n-not scared!" croaked the man

as he backed away.

P. King snarled. "Well, you should be…"

In a flash, the two geese were at the man's side, leading him away down a dark alley.

"For The Drake!" yelled Colonel P. King.

"For The Drake!" repeated all the soldiers and bystanders.

"Company, quick waddle!"

The platoon once again set off on their parade, bills pointed dead ahead.

"What will happen to that man?" Luke whispered.

"He'll be sent to the Bakery for daring to stand up to them," said Jasmine. "Come on, we'd better get this information through to Dad."

Making sure no one could see them, Jasmine and Luke clambered out of the bushes and made their way into a nearby back garden. At the end of the overgrown lawn was a tumbledown shed. The pair hurried inside.

Luke switched on the old two-way radio and adjusted the frequency. "Little

Boy calling Big Man," he said into the microphone. "Come in, Big Man — we have an update for you."

Chapter Three:
Beardy

In a large country mansion less than a mile away, Professor Douglas Viccars leaned his elbows on the edge of the war room table, and sighed. Sometimes it was hard to believe that he was surrounded by the greatest minds human society had to offer.

"No, no, no!" roared the Prime Minister from the other end of the table. "We have been over this again and again — for weeks now! The ducks must be dealt with by any means possible. If that requires the use of flame-throwers, then we'll just have to have a big old barbecue as a celebration feast!"

"Hear, hear!" said the head of the Secret Service. "Fry 'em to a crisp!"

"Burn 'em all!" exclaimed the King.

"And then add some rice!" said the Archbishop, licking her lips.

The Prime Minister held up his hand for quiet. His eyes swept the people sitting around the vast table. "This war council — the only thing standing between the ducks and humankind — must all agree on whichever course of action we decide to take, or it's back to the drawing board."

The assembled figures mumbled their understanding.

"So," said the PM, "the motion on the table is that we use fire as a way to stop the ducks from taking over the planet. All in favour, raise your hand..."

Professor Viccars counted the number of voters and jotted it down. "21," he said.

The Prime Minister swallowed hard. "And those against..."

One single, solitary hand shot into the air. Everyone else groaned.

"Oh, no!"

"Not again!"

"I knew it!"

The Prime Minister took off his glasses and rubbed his tired eyes. "Mr Beardy," he said. "It appears you have once again voted against the wishes of the entire war council."

A small, untidy man with a beard and tiny round glasses wobbled to his feet. "Indeed I did!" cried Bill Beardy. "And I'll tell you all why..."

There was another room-wide groan.

"I was afraid he might," grumbled the Chief of Police.

"Here we go again..." muttered a Navy Admiral.

Bill Beardy took no notice of the comments. He reached into one of the many pockets of his jacket and pulled out a battered old book of bird species. "Many of you will know me from my popular TV shows about nature," he began. "There's *Worm Watch*, *Mole Follower* and *Butterfly Stalker* to name but a few..."

"We're all aware of your credentials as a beloved TV naturalist, Mr Beardy," said the Prime Minister. "Please get to your point!"

Bill Beardy opened his book to the entry about mallard ducks. "These were what ducks looked like until recently," he said. "But now, they've changed. They've evolved! They are an entirely new breed of waterfowl and they must be protected at all costs! You can't go wading in there with great big flame-throwers! There's a chance some of the little quackers might get hurt."

"He's bonkers!" said the Admiral.

"Out of his tiny, beardy mind!" commented the Archbishop.

"Mr Beardy!" said the Prime Minister through gritted teeth. "These ducks have not evolved — we did this to them! Months of feeding them bread laced with Omega 33 turned them into big-brained, nasty, duck-stepping—"

A red light began to flash on a console in the middle of the table.

"It's the ducks!" screamed the King, diving underneath the table. "We're doomed!"

"It's not the ducks!" said Professor Viccars, snatching up a headset and slipping it over his ears. "It's my children, and they have a report to make..."

Chapter Four:
Bakery

Luke checked the volume on the radio handset, making sure it wasn't loud enough to be heard by anyone who happened to be passing the garden fence.

"This is Big Man to Little Boy," hissed the speaker. "Are you certain it was Colonel P. King and the Dabbler platoon you saw in town?"

"That's what Little Girl told me," said Luke.

Jasmine nodded. "It was definitely him."

There was a slight pause.

"Then we need to bring Operation Bake-Off forward to today," said Professor Viccars. "Do you understand what that means?"

Luke and Jasmine exchanged a determined glance. "Operation Bake-Off is go!" confirmed Luke. "Over and out." Luke switched off the radio set and sat back in his chair.

Jasmine reached into her bag and pulled out a glass bottle containing a vivid purple liquid. "I guess it's time to go to work, then," she said with a smile.

The pair hurried out of the shed and made

their way back to the street. The crowds had disappeared now that the duck parade had passed. They crossed the road and were about to head down the alley where earlier the geese had dragged their prisoner, when a group of boys and girls stepped in front of them. They were dressed in grey uniforms and green balaclavas.

"Halt!" bellowed the largest boy, performing the ducks' salute. "For The Drake!"

"For The Drake!" cried his gang, copying the move.

"Well, look who it is…" said Jasmine. "The Mallard Youth!"

"The very same!" said the boy. "And I couldn't help but notice that you didn't salute back to us!"

"You don't have to salute," Luke pointed out. "It's not the law or anything."

"It will be very soon," growled the boy. "And when it is—"

"I'm sure you'll be even more pleased with your duck-loving self than you are right now," finished Jasmine.

The boy scowled. "What's in the bag,"
he demanded.

"Nothing at all to do with you," said
Jasmine.

"And what if I take it off you by force?"

Jasmine fixed her eyes on the Mallard Youth leader. "I'd like to see you try..." she said quietly, keeping her opponent's gaze.

There was an awkward silence, after which the boy gave a forced laugh. "It's probably just kids' stuff anyway!" he barked.

"Come on, Luke. This lot look like they're coming *down* with something," said Jasmine, sniggering.

"Yeah, they should see a ducktor!" grinned Luke, hurrying into the alley after his sister.

The grey-suited goons pulled faces behind their backs, then marched clumsily away.

At the far end of the alley, Luke and

Jasmine came to a metal chain-link fence.

"This is it," Jasmine hissed. "The Bakery!"

Luke looked up at the huge building.
"This is where human slaves are forced to
bake bread with Omega 33 in for the ducks?"

Jasmine nodded. "It is until we put a stop
to it," she said.

With the help of a wire-cutter, the children were soon creeping through the grounds of the Bakery. Luke picked the lock on a side door, and the pair slipped inside.

They found themselves in a large room. Tired-looking men and women were pouring ingredients into huge mixing bowls, kneading dough and sliding uncooked loaves of bread into giant ovens.

"There!" whispered Jasmine, pointing to a man pouring a bright green liquid into the bread mix. "That's where the Omega 33 goes in!"

"So that's where we have to dump our stuff," said Luke, retrieving the bottle of purple fluid and staring into it.

"Be careful," said Jasmine. She took the potion from her brother. "That's powerful stuff, and we need every drop of it. It's pure Omega Minus 34!"

Chapter Five:
Bread

Professor Viccars slid off his headset. "It's done," he said. "Teams are now in action at every bakery around the world. Operation Bake-Off has begun."

Bill Beardy frowned. "Operation Bake-Off?" he said.

"Our Plan B, Mr Beardy," said the Prime Minister. "All you have done is vote against every plan we came up with to stop the ducks — we knew we had to act without you."

Bill Beardy scanned the faces of everyone else at the table. They were all smirking. "You went behind my back?" he roared. "This is unbelievable!"

"We had no choice!" shouted the Prime Minister.

"But, the new breed of ducks..." said Bill Beardy.

"They will not be harmed in any way," said Professor Viccars. "All we are doing is reversing the polarity of their food."

Bill Beardy blinked blankly. "How?"

"We are contaminating the bread made in the slave bakeries with a mixture I've made called Omega Minus 34," the Professor explained.

"But that means the ducks will revert back to normal!" Beardy gasped.

"More than that," grinned the Professor. "My potion has a negative effect. Ducks all over the world will become even more dim-witted than they were before."

"But The Drake!" blustered Beardy. "He won't stand for it!"

"He will have no choice!" the PM pointed

out. "Our human operatives are at work as we speak, pouring bottles of precious Omega Minus 34 into the bread mixture!"

"NOOO!" screeched Bill Beardy, slumping back into his seat.

"Strange man," said the Navy Admiral.

"Certainly is," added the Chief of Police.

"Almost as though he wants the ducks to win," said the King from under the table.

Back at the Bakery, Jasmine poured purple liquid into the bread mix. "That dough has now got Omega 33 and Omega Minus 34 in it."

"Making a grand total of minus one," said Luke. "Dumb ducks, here we come!"

"We'd better get out of here," whispered Jasmine.

But, then...

"Hey, I know you two!"

Luke and Jasmine spun round to find the middle-aged man from the street smiling down at them. He was wearing white baker's clothes and carrying a tray of freshly baked bread. "You were in the bushes when I stood up to the ducks!"

"How do you know?" asked Jasmine.

"I was hiding in there with you for an hour until the parade came along," the man admitted. "What are you doing here?"

"Putting a stop to the ducks once and for all," said Luke.

"Oh, that's great!" beamed the man. "Then you can arrest The Drake at the same time!"

"The Drake?" hissed Jasmine. "He's here?"

"So the others say," nodded the man. "His nest is hidden down in the sewers."

A duck guard waddled past. Luke and Jasmine quickly "ducked" behind the mixing bowl. "Hey you, get back to work!" the mallard cried to the man.

"Yes, sir!" said the new baker. He winked at the children, then hurried away.

Luke took a deep breath. "We won't get another chance like this," he said.

"I know," agreed Jasmine. "Let's get down to the sewers!"

Taking care to avoid the green-headed guards, the pair made their way through the bread factory and down into the sewers. There, at the end of one of the tunnels, a large duck sat on a nest of leaves. And he was looking the other way!

"We can creep up on him!" mouthed Luke.

The children moved as silently as they could, edging closer and closer to the nest, until...

"Gotcha!" cried Luke, snatching up The Drake.

SQUEAK!

"That's not him!" exclaimed Jasmine.

"It's a rubber duck bath toy! A decoy!"

Luke frowned. "Then where is the real

Drake?"

Chapter Six:
Battle

ZZZZIIIIPPPPP!

It was fair to say that no one in the war room had ever seen anyone unzip the back of their head before — but Bill Beardy was doing that right now!

"That's horrible!" gulped the Prime Minister.

"Disgusting!" agreed the Archbishop.

"I've just peed my pants!" sobbed the King.

The zip undone, Bill Beardy reached up and pulled off his mask. Everyone in the room gasped as they found themselves staring at a mallard duck with a moustache.

"You're The Drake!" exclaimed the Prime Minister.

"Actually, I'm The Drake balanced on top of six other ducks," The Drake replied.

"Can we come out now?" asked one of the lower birds.

"Hush!" said The Drake to the lower part of Bill Beardy's body.

"No wonder you always voted against us!" said the Chief of Police.

"He's one of them!" wheezed the Archbishop.

"*The* one of them!" confirmed the head of the Secret Service.

"Silence!" quacked The Drake. "You fed us bread, now we want you dead!"

"It's too late," said the Professor. "My new bread is dumbing your soldiers down already..."

He gestured out of the window where Colonel P. King and his Dabbler Platoon were staggering around in circles.

"Bah!" scoffed The Drake. "But it's not too late for me... Not if you call your children and order them to put triple the amount of Omega 33 into my personal batch of bread!"

"But... But... That would be Omega 99!" spluttered the PM.

"Exactly!" sneered The Drake. "I will become the most intelligent creature the planet has ever seen. The future will be mine to rule as I wish."

"We won't do it!" wailed the King.

"Yes, you will," said The Drake. "And, just to make sure you all comply, I've put a pair of guards outside..."

The war room doors creaked open to reveal a pair of large, vicious-looking geese. One had an eye patch, and both had tattoos on their wings.

"Make the call, Professor Viccars," said The Drake as the doors closed again. "Or none of you will get out of this room in one piece."

"I can't make the call," said the Professor with a smile.

The Drake blinked. "And why not?"

Professor Viccars pointed to the flashing red light on the radio in the middle of the table. "The line is already live," he said. "My children have heard every single word! This is Big Man to Little Boy and Little Girl — do it now!"

The doors crashed open and Jasmine and Luke charged in, leaping over a pair of unconscious geese. They were both holding brightly coloured super-soaker water guns.

"Your weapons are useless!" sneered The Drake. "It will be water off a duck's back!"

"It would," said Jasmine, "if these were

filled with water…"

The green feathers of The Drake's cheeks paled a little. "So, what is in there?"

"The rest of my dad's supply of Omega Minus 34!" hollered Luke, then both children began to squirt.

The Drake was knocked off his perch as the purple liquid drenched him. With a terrible squawk, he tumbled to the floor as the ducks beneath him were drenched and stupidity washed over them.

"Did it work?" asked the King.

"Well, check it!" exclaimed the PM.

Professor Viccars hurried around the room and gently lifted the duck with the moustache onto the table.

"Well?" he said. "What do you have to say for yourself?"

The Drake looked up at the assembled crowd with dull eyes, opened his beak and said...

"Moo!"

Chapter Seven: Bingo

"I knew you'd grow to like playing bingo!" said Norah, settling down onto the bench by the pond.

"Well, it beats being chased around by ducks! I'm glad they're all back in the pond," said Tom. "Now, where's the bread?"

Norah pulled a stale loaf from her bag.

Tom tore off a lump and tossed it out into the water. In the middle of the pond, the ducks were swimming about aimlessly, occasionally bumping into each other and mooing.

"None of that Omega rubbish, I hope," he said.

"Not a bit of it," said Norah. "It says on the bag that it's a new recipe." She watched as two ducks tussled over a piece of crust. One with a weedy moustache lost out and slowly swam off, mooing quietly.

Once again, the elderly pair fell into a comfortable silence as they fed the ducks. The sun was sinking in the sky, and a gentle breeze rustled the leaves on the trees.

In fact, everything was so perfect that neither of them noticed a frog hop out of the water and onto a lily pad. It shot out its tongue to grab a piece of bread, scoffed it down, and then began to rub its tiny palms together and croak wickedly...